Louis Kinney Harlow

The Everlasting Hills

Louis Kinney Harlow

The Everlasting Hills

ISBN/EAN: 9783337108595

Printed in Europe, USA, Canada, Australia, Japan

Cover: Foto ©Andreas Hilbeck / pixelio.de

More available books at **www.hansebooks.com**

THE
Everlasting Hills.

BY
Louis K. Harlow

BOSTON,
SAMUEL E. CASSINO.

I cried unto the Lord with my voice,
and he heard me out of his holy hill.

PSALMS, III, 4.

1st Day

Far upward in the mellow light
Rose the blue hills. One cloud of white,
Around a far uplifted cone.
In the warm blush of evening shone;
An image of the silver lakes,
By which the Indian's soul awakes.

HENRY W. LONGFELLOW.

2nd Day

I stood upon the hills, when heaven's wide arch
Was glorious with the sun's returning march,
And woods were brightened, and soft gales
Went forth to kiss the sun-clad vales.
The clouds were far beneath me;
                    bathed in light.

HENRY W. LONGFELLOW.

3rd Day

You never get to the end of Christ's words.
There is something in them always behind.
They pass into proverbs, they pass into laws,
they pass into doctrines, they pass into consol-
ations; but they never pass away; and after
all the use that is made of them, they are
still not exhausted.

DEAN STANLEY.

4th Day

The high hills are a refuge for
the wild goats, and the rocks
for the conies.

PSALMS.CIV.18.

5.th Day

When winter winds are piercing chill,
And through the hawthorn blows the gale,
With solemn feet I tread the hill,
That everbrows the lonely vale.

HENRY W. LONGFELLOW.

6th Day

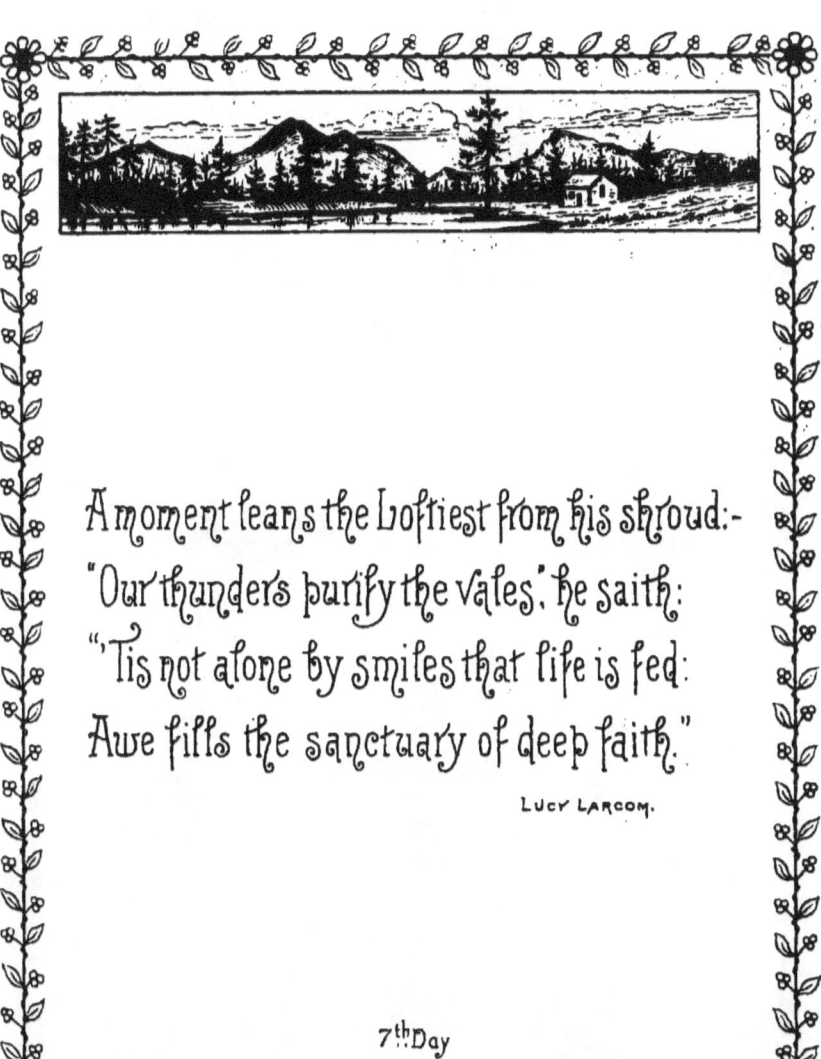

A moment leans the Loftiest from his shroud:-
"Our thunders purify the vales", he saith:
",Tis not alone by smiles that life is fed:
Awe fills the sanctuary of deep faith."

LUCY LARCOM.

7th Day

Exalt the Lord our God, and worship at
his holy hill : for the Lord our God is holy.

PSALMS, xcix, 9.

8th Day

The fresh, bracing air of the Spirit is always to be found on the hills of Truth. A good ramble over the heights and depths of the Word, its hills and dales, its hidden glens and gorges, its green pastures and its still waters, is the best tonic for the drooping soul. Spiritual roses in the cheek are to be got in this way. That soul retains a clear eye and a good complexion who lives much in the open air of the Word.

CAROLINE FOX.

9th Day

Mountains, and all hills; fruitful
trees, and all cedars :

PSALMS. CXLVIII, 9.

10th Day

If thou art worn and hard beset
With sorrows, that thou wouldst forget,
If thou wouldst read a lesson, that will keep
Thy heart from fainting, and thy soul from sleep,
Go to the woods and hills! No tears
Dim the sweet look that Nature wears.

HENRY W. LONGFELLOW.

11th Day

Yet have I set my King upon my
holy hill of Zion.

PSALMS, 11, 6.

12th Day

The blessings of thy father have prevailed above the blessings of my progenitors, unto the utmost bound of the everlasting hills: they shall be on the head of Joseph, and on the crown of head of him that was separate from his brethren.

GENESIS, XLIX, 26.

13th Day

He sendeth the springs into the valleys,
which run among the hills.

PSALMS, CIV, 10.

14th Day

For the mountains shall depart, and
the hills be removed; but my kindness
shall not depart from thee, neither
shall the covenant of my peace be
removed, saith the Lord that hath
mercy on thee.

ISAIAH, LIV, 10

15th Day

Once, I know, I shall journey far,
Over the mountains high.
Lord, is thy door already ajar?
Dear is the home where my loved ones are;
But bar it a while from me,
And help me to long for thee.

B·B·JOHNSON·

16th Day

I will have hopes that cannot fade,
For flowers the valley yields;
I will have quiet thoughts, instead
Of silent, dewy fields;
My Spirit and my God shall be
My seaward Hill, my boundless sea.

E. B. BROWNING.

17th Day

Let the floods clap their hands:
let the hills be joyful together.

PSALMS, XCVIII, 8.

18th Day

The hills were covered with
the shadow of it, and the boughs
thereof were like the goodly cedars.

PSALMS. LXXX, 10.

19th Day

Every valley shall be exalted, and
every mountain and hill shall be made
low: and the crooked shall be made
straight, and the rough places plain.

ISAIAH, XL, 4.

20th Day

O'er all the hill-tops
Is quiet now,
In all the tree-tops
Hearest thou
Hardly a breath;
The birds are asleep in the trees:
Wait; soon like these
Thou, too, shalt rest.

HENRY W. LONGFELLOW.

21st Day

O silent hills across the lake,
Asleep in moonlight, or awake
To catch the color of the sky,
That sifts through every cloud swept by,

LUCY LARCOM.

22nd Day

The mountains shall bring peace to the people,
and the little hills, by righteousness.

PSALMS. lxx, 3

23rd Day

They drop upon the pastures of the wilderness; and the little hills rejoice on every side.

PSALMS, lxv. 12.

24th Day

Rills that start
From this Hill's bosom, there reflect the sky,
And his deep shadows greener grace impart
To the sweet fields which low beneath him lie.

LUCY LARCOM.

25th Day

In his hand are the deep places of the earth;
the strength of the hills is his also.

PSALMS, XCV, 4.

26th Day

And for the chief things of the ancient mountains, and for the precious things of the lasting hills.

DEUTERONOMY, XXXIII, 15.

27th Day

I will lift up mine eyes unto the hills,
from whence cometh my help.

PSALMS. CXXI, 1.

28ᵗʰ Day

I stand on high,
　　　Close to the sky,
Kissed by unsullied lips of light;
　　　Fanned by soft airs
　　　That seem like prayers
Floating to God through ether bright.

C. G. AMES.

Lord, who shall abide in thy tabernacle?
who shall dwell in thy holy hill?

PSALMS, XV, I.

30th Day

The contemplation of celestial things will make a man both speak and think more sublimely and magnificently when he descends to human affairs.

CICERO.

31st Day

www.ingramcontent.com/pod-product-compliance
Lightning Source LLC
Chambersburg PA
CBHW021228260626
47172CB00002B/657